THE
SHERLOCK
HOLMES

CHILDREN'S COLLECTION

SHADOWS, SECRETS AND STOLEN TREASURE

Published by Sweet Cherry Publishing Limited
Unit 36, Vulcan House,
Vulcan Road,
Leicester, LE5 3EF
United Kingdom

First published in the UK in 2019
2019 edition

2 4 6 8 10 9 7 5 3 1

ISBN: 978-1-78226-417-0

© Sweet Cherry Publishing

Sherlock Holmes: The Veiled Lodger

Cover Design by Arianna Bellucci and Rhiannon Izard
Illustrations by Arianna Bellucci

www.sweetcherrypublishing.com

Printed and bound in China
C.WM004

SHERLOCK HOLMES

THE VEILED LODGER

SIR ARTHUR CONAN DOYLE

Sweet
Cherry
PUBLISHING

For seventeen of the twenty-
three years that Sherlock
Holmes worked as a consulting
detective, I assisted him with
his investigations. In that time
he took on hundreds of cases,
all of which
had proved to
be beyond the
abilities of
the police.

Since he delighted in investigating the bizarre and seemingly unexplainable, each case has aspects that would make for fascinating reading. The problem is not lack of material, but which of our investigations to choose. Also Holmes took on such high-profile cases, that there are many I am bound to keep secret in order to protect the honour of those involved.

Over the years Holmes has

received many
letters from people
concerned that the
honour and reputation
of their families would
suffer were these stories
made public. There is
nothing to fear. My friend
has always been known for
his tact and trustworthiness.
No secrets will be revealed.
However, I must condemn the
recent attempts at destroying
Holmes' case notes. If such

for you. Ot must appreciat matter is hia and could a my standi details e

actions continue, I have his blessing to release the story of the politician, the lighthouse and the trained cormorant to the public. There is at least one reader who will understand.

Not all of the cases Holmes was involved in allowed him to demonstrate the remarkable gifts of instinct and observation that I have attempted to highlight in these memoirs. The story I now wish to tell is one such mystery. It contains such tragedy that I cannot in good conscience keep it from the public. I have changed the names and places in order to protect the identities of those involved in this dark business.

It was one morning late in 1896 that I received a hurried note from Holmes asking that I come to Baker Street immediately.

Watson,

Please come to Baker Street at once. Your presence may be of great help.

Sherlock

When I arrived I found him seated before the fire with an elderly, motherly woman in the chair opposite him. I studied her and attempted to deduce her circumstances, as Holmes often did with his clients. She was dressed respectably in a dark woollen dress, which was clean and bore no patches, but it was clearly some years old. Whoever she was, it was clear to me that even though she struggled for money, she took great pride in her appearance. Her boots were polished and, as she removed the bonnet from her head, I saw that she wore no wedding ring, so had no husband to support her. I tried to imagine how she earned her money. Her hands did not have the roughness of a laundress, yet neither was she a lady's maid. A cook, perhaps? She had the look of someone used to physical work. I could at once see her up to her elbows in flour as she baked the bread for the household.

'This is Mrs Merrilow, of South Brixton,' said my friend, with a wave of his hand.

Brixton, too, fitted my deductions.

South Brixton
Part of Lambeth. Very mixed in terms of class – residents range from dockmen and labourers to rich businessmen. Many of the grand villas have since been converted into boarding houses.

There were many grand houses there in which I was certain she could be employed. With a nod and smile towards our visitor, I focused my attention on the discussion at hand, confident that she would now confirm my theories.

'Mrs Merrilow is a landlady, much like our own Mrs Hudson. She has an interesting story to tell that may well lead to further developments in which your presence may be useful.'

'Anything I can do,' I said, drawing up a chair and seating myself between them. I was glad that I had not shared my theories with Holmes, but embarrassment at my error

must have shown on my face.
Holmes gave me a quizzical
look before turning back to the
lady.

'You will understand, Mrs
Merrilow, that if I come to Mrs
Ronder I should prefer to have
a witness to our conversation.
You must make her understand
that before Watson and I arrive.'

'Bless you, Mr Holmes,' said
our visitor. 'She is so anxious to
see you that you could bring the
whole city with you!'

'Then we shall come early this afternoon. Let us see that we have our facts correct before we start. If we go over them it will help Doctor Watson to understand the situation. You say that Mrs Ronder has been your lodger for seven years and that you have only once seen her face.'

'That is correct, sir. And I wish that I had not,' said Mrs Merrilow.

'It was, I understand, terribly mutilated.'

'Well, Mr Holmes, you would hardly say it was a face at all. That's how it looked. Our milkman got a glimpse of her once, peeping out of the upper window, and it gave him such a fright that he dropped his milk all over the front garden.

That is the kind of face it is. A few weeks later I happened to come up the stairs just as she was returning to her room. She covered up quick as soon as she saw me, and then she said, "Now, Mrs Merrilow, you know at last why it is that I never raise my veil."'

'Do you know anything about her history?'

'Nothing at all.'

'Did she give references when she came?'

'No, sir, but she gave hard cash, and plenty of it. Three

months' rent right down on the table in advance and no arguing about my terms. In these times a poor woman like me can't afford to turn down a chance like that.'

'Did she give any reason for choosing your house?'

Mrs Merrilow shook her head slightly and answered without hesitation. 'She didn't, but I think I might know why she settled on my house. It stands well back from the road

and the garden makes it more
private than most. Also, I only
take one lodger at a time, and
I have no family of my own. I
reckon she had tried others and
found that mine suited her best.

20

It's privacy she's after, and she is willing to pay for it.'

Holmes nodded, his keen eyes glittering. The lady's logic was undeniable and my friend was clearly impressed with her observations.

'You say that she never showed her face at all except on that one accidental occasion. Well, it is a very remarkable story, and I am not at all surprised that you want it examined.'

'I don't, Mr Holmes! I am quite satisfied so long as I get my rent. You could not wish for a quieter lodger, or one who gives less trouble.'

'Then what has caused you to come to me?'

Our visitor looked my friend directly in the eye with an expression of deep concern. 'Her health, Mr Holmes. The poor lady seems to be wasting away. And there's something terrible on her

mind. "Murder!" she cries.
"Murder!" And once I heard
her shout, "You cruel beast!
You monster!" It was in the
night, and it fair rang through
the house and sent the shivers
through me. So I went to her
in the morning. "Mrs Ronder,"
I says, "if you have anything
that's troubling your soul, I
can call a church minister or
priest," I says, "and there's the
police. One of them should be
able to help you."

'"For God's sake, not the police!" she says. "And no minister can change what is past. And yet," she says, "it would ease my mind if someone knew the truth before I died."

'"Well," says I, "if you won't consider a priest or the police, there is this detective man what we read about" – beggin' your pardon, Mr Holmes. And she jumped at it.'

'"That's the man," says she. "I cannot believe I never thought of it before. Bring him here, Mrs Merrilow, and if he won't come, tell him I am the wife of Ronder's wild beast show. Say that, and give him the name Abbas Parva." Here it is, just as she wrote it. She says, "That will bring him, if he's the man I think he is."'

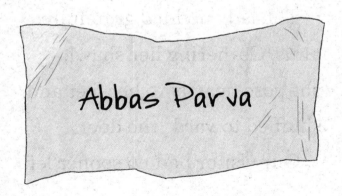

Abbas Parva

'And it will, too,' remarked Holmes. 'Very good, Mrs Merrilow. I think that is all I need. I should like to have a little chat with Dr Watson first. I should think that will take us until lunchtime. You may expect to see us at your house in Brixton at about three o'clock.'

The lady nodded gratefully at us. Gathering her shawl, she rose heavily to her feet and shuffled towards the door.

Our visitor had no sooner left

the room than Holmes pulled down several books from his disordered bookshelf in the corner and spread them on the floor. Then he threw himself upon them with fierce energy, and for the next few minutes the only sound was a constant swish of pages. Finally, Holmes gave a grunt of satisfaction when he found what he was looking for.

He was so excited that he did not return to his chair. Instead he remained sitting on the floor with crossed legs, the huge books all around him, and one open upon his knees.

Without looking up from the volume in his lap, Holmes spoke. 'Here it is. This case puzzled me at the time, Watson. Here are my notes in the margin to prove it. I admit that I could make nothing of it, and yet I was convinced that the coroner was wrong. Do you not remember the Abbas Parva tragedy?'

'Not at all, Holmes,' I said, twisting in my chair to look at my friend.

'And yet we had been sharing these rooms for quite a while by that time.' He shook his head with a sigh. No doubt he was despairing at my inability to recall the details of the case, as usual. I merely rolled my eyes and waited for him to continue.

'I was not able to conduct a full investigation, for none of the people involved had engaged my services. With nothing to guide an investigation, I was forced to give it up. However, the mystery has continued to fascinate me and I often find myself turning it over in my mind. Perhaps you would care to read the notes I have here?'

'Could you just give me the main points?'

'That's very easily done. It will probably come back to your memory as I talk. Ronder, of course, was a household name. He was the owner of one of the largest circuses in the country, and one of the greatest showmen of his day. There is evidence, however, that he took to drinking and that both he and his show were in decline at the time of the great tragedy.

'I believe the incident happened during a tour of the country. The caravans had halted for the night at Abbas Parva, which is a small village in Berkshire, when this horror occurred. They were on their way to Wimbledon,

---

Circus
Shows featuring animal acts, acrobatics and comedy. Modern shows travel around the country with performances in a tent called a 'big top'. There have been instances of wild animals escaping such shows, as in the St George's Street incident of 1857. Thankfully these are rare occurrences.

travelling by road, and stopped
there simply to camp. There
was no show that night, since
Abbas Parva is so small that it
wouldn't have been worth the
money for them to open.

'They had a very fine North
African lion among their
exhibits. Sahara King was its
name. Ronder and his wife
had an act that involved them
entering its cage where they
would give performances.
Here, you see, is a photograph

of their show. You will notice that Ronder was a huge man and that his wife was a very magnificent woman.'

I leaned over to take a look at the photo Holmes was holding. It was grainy but I could see the three figures on it: the lion standing proudly with its mouth open in a snarl; Ronder, holding a whip; and his wife standing beside him. Mrs Ronder was holding up her arms as if commanding the

animal to perform. Although she was much smaller than her giant husband, her beauty caught my eye. Her costume, a typical show dress, sparkled in the show lights.

As I studied the photograph, Holmes continued. 'It was usual for either Ronder or his wife to feed the lion at night. Sometimes one went, sometimes both, but they never allowed anyone else to do it. They believed that as long as they were the food carriers, the animal would see them as friendly and not attack them. Interestingly, it was stated at the enquiry that there had been some signs that the lion was in fact dangerous. However, it seems these signs had been ignored. I suspect that the couple had become so familiar with the lion that they no longer believed it could do them any harm.

'On this particular night, seven years ago, they both went to do the feeding. A very terrible happening followed, the details of which have never been made clear.'

I seemed to vaguely recall the story now. Perhaps I had read about it in the newspaper at the time. With a sinking heart, I dreaded what was to come.

Holmes went on. 'It seems that the whole camp was roused at about midnight by the roars of the animal and the screams of the woman. The grooms and employees rushed from their tents, carrying lanterns, and the lights revealed an awful sight.

Ronder lay, with the back of
his head crushed and deep
claw marks across his scalp,
about ten yards from the cage,
which was open. Close to
the door of the cage lay Mrs
Ronder on her back, with the
creature squatting and
snarling above her. It

had savaged her face in such
a fashion that no one present
imagined that she could live.

'Several of the circus men,
headed by Leonardo,
the strongman, and
Griggs, the clown,
drove the creature
off with poles.

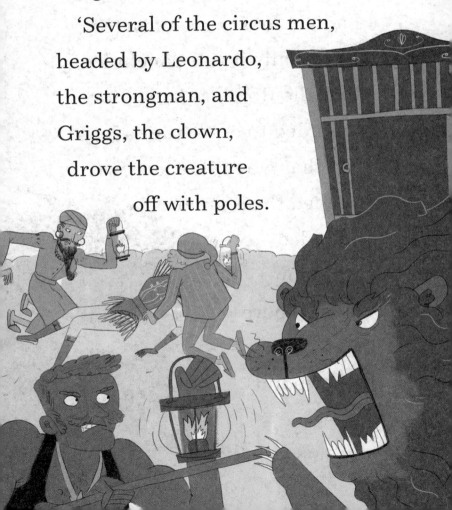

The men managed to get the
lion back into its cage and it
was at once locked in. How it
had got loose was a mystery.
Eventually it was concluded
that the Ronders had
intended to enter the cage,
but that when the door was
opened the animal
bounded
out upon
them. There
was no
other point

of interest in the evidence, except that Mrs Ronder, in agony, kept screaming, "Coward! Coward!" as she was carried away. It was six months before she was fit to give evidence, and then the investigation into the death of her husband was held. The obvious verdict was accidental death.'

'What other could there be?' I said.

'You may well say so,' Holmes

went on. 'And yet there were one or two points that worried young Edmunds, of the Berkshire Constabulary. A smart lad that! A rarity among policemen. Although the case was closed, Edmunds was not satisfied with the verdict and dropped into my rooms one day to ask for my thoughts on it. We had a very lively discussion about it, although neither of us could come up with a satisfactory theory.

Surely you must remember him?'

Something nagged at my memory. 'A thin, yellow-haired man?'

'Exactly. I was sure you would remember eventually.'

Even after all our years together, Holmes still took great delight in teasing me as I struggled to catch up. I determined that I wouldn't react and instead asked, 'But what worried him?'

'Well, we were both worried. It was so difficult to reconstruct the affair. Look at it from the lion's point of view. The cage door is open. He is free. What does he do? He takes half a dozen bounds forward, which brings him to Ronder. Ronder turns to run – the claw marks were on the *back* of his head – but the lion strikes him down. Then, instead of bounding on and escaping, he returns to the woman who was close to the cage, and he knocks her over and attacks her savagely. Why would the lion not escape to freedom when he had the chance?

'To add to the mystery, the unfortunate lady's cries suggested that her husband had in some way failed her. But what could the poor devil have possibly done to help her? You see the difficulty?'

'Quite.'

'And then there was another thing. It comes back to me

now as I think it over. There was some evidence that just as the lion roared and the woman screamed, a man began shouting in terror.'

'This man Ronder, no doubt.'

'Well, if his skull was smashed in you would hardly expect to hear from him again, would you? There were at least two witnesses who mentioned the cries of a man being mingled with those of a woman. By the time the lion attacked

Mrs Ronder, her husband was already dead.'

'I should think the whole camp was crying out by then,' I said. 'As to the other points, I think I could suggest a solution.'

Holmes looked at me down his nose in that superior way he had. 'I would be glad to hear it.'

I decided to ignore his sarcasm.

This mystery had also captured my imagination and I was determined to have my say.

'The two were together, ten yards from the cage, when the lion got loose. The man turned to run away and was struck down. The woman had the idea of getting into the cage and shutting the door. It was her only chance. She made for the cage, and just as she reached it, the beast bounded after her and knocked her over. She was angry at her husband for having encouraged the lion's rage by turning away. If they had faced it, they might have intimidated it. Hence her cries of "Coward!"'

'Brilliant, Watson! Only one flaw in your story.'

I tried not to let my irritation show but I suspect Holmes was well aware of my feelings. Nevertheless, I looked him in the eye.

'What is the flaw, Holmes?'

'If they were both ten yards from the cage, how did the beast get out?'

I hadn't considered that. I fell into silence for a moment as I mulled over the possibilities.

'Is it possible that they had some enemy who unlocked it?'

'And why should it attack them so savagely when it was in the habit of playing with them and doing tricks with them inside the cage? They were the ones who fed it, don't forget.'

'Possibly the same enemy had done something to enrage it.'

Holmes looked thoughtful and remained in silence for some moments.

I knew my argument was weak. I prepared myself for Holmes' scorn and was

pleasantly surprised when
Holmes said, 'Well, Watson,
there is this to be said for your
theory. Ronder was a
man of many
enemies.
Edmunds told
me that he was
horrible. A
huge bully of a
man who cursed and
threatened violence at
anyone who came in
his way. I expect those

56

cries about a monster, of which our visitor has spoken, were Mrs Ronder's memories of her late husband. However, until we have all the facts, all we can do is speculate.'

He returned to his state of deep thought and stared into the fire for a moment before jumping to his feet and clapping his hands together. 'There is a cold partridge on the sideboard, Watson, and a bottle of wine. Let us renew our energies before we

call upon this tragic woman and
her landlady.'

Some sixty minutes later,
when our hansom cab dropped
us at Mrs Merrilow's house,
we found that lady standing in
the doorway waiting for us. It
was very clear that her main
concern was that she should
not lose a valuable source of
income. Before she showed us
upstairs she begged us to say or
do nothing that could lead to
her lodger leaving.

Having spent a good few minutes attempting to reassure her, we followed her up the straight, badly carpeted staircase and were shown into the room of the mysterious lodger. We entered and I was aware of Mrs Merrilow standing beside me, clearly anxious, although whether for herself or her lodger I could not tell. She twisted a handkerchief in her hands and shifted her weight from one foot to the other, making the floorboards creak under the worn carpet. Holmes must have been aware of her restlessness too, because he turned and raised an eyebrow. This was enough to bring the good lady back to her senses. With a sheepish glance, she left the room and we heard her heavy steps as she returned downstairs.

It was a musty and poorly ventilated place, as might be expected since its occupant rarely left it. As I looked around, it became obvious that the room was badly in need of some attention. The wallpaper had begun to peel in places and there were thick layers of dust on the mantelpiece. I noticed that there were no ornaments or personal belongings on display, and the whole room suggested an atmosphere of misery. It looked like a room that nobody lived in. I saw the irony in the fact that, from once keeping beasts in a cage, the woman seemed to have become a beast in a cage herself.

The lady we had been

summoned to see sat in a broken
armchair in a shadowy corner
of the room. I could see that
she had once been a very active
woman, but many years of
inactivity had caused her figure
to soften somewhat.

A thick, dark veil covered her face, but it was cut off close to her upper lip, showing a perfectly shaped mouth and a delicately rounded chin. I could easily believe that she had been a very remarkable woman. Her voice, too, was pleasant on the ear.

'Mr Holmes,' she said by way of a greeting. 'My name is familiar to you, I see.

I thought that it would bring you.'

'That is so, madam, though I do not know how you were aware that I was interested in your case.'

'I learned it when I had recovered my health after the mauling by Sahara King. I was being examined by Mr Edmunds, the county detective. I fear I lied to him. Perhaps it would have been better if I had told the truth.'

'It is usually wiser to tell the truth. But why did you lie to him?'

'Because the fate of someone else depended upon my statement. I know that he was a very worthless being, and yet I did not want his destruction on my conscience. We had been so close – so close.'

'Has this obstacle been removed, then?'

'Yes, sir. The person I am referring to is dead.'

'Then why haven't you told the police what you know?'

'Because there is another person to be considered. That other person is myself. I could not stand the scandal and publicity that would come from a police examination. I have not long to live, but I wish to die undisturbed. And yet I also wanted to find one man of judgement to whom I could tell my terrible story, so that when I am gone all might be understood.'

'You compliment me, madam. At the same time, I am a responsible person. I cannot promise you that when you have spoken I may not think it my duty to report it to the police.'

'I think not, Mr Holmes. I know your character and methods too well, for I have followed your work for some years. Reading is the only pleasure

that fate has left me, and I
miss little that happens in the
world. But in any case, I will
tell you, Mr Holmes. Then you
can do what you wish with the
information. It will ease my
mind to tell it.'

'My friend Doctor Watson
and I would be glad to hear it.'

'Then please be seated,
gentlemen.'

We did so. Holmes pulled
up a chair opposite her and I
sat discreetly to one side. As

desperate as I was to learn the dark secret that hung around this lady, I realised that we had to be patient and allow her to tell her story.

She rose suddenly and took two framed photographs from a drawer.

'This is Leonardo,' she said, handing one of them to Holmes. I leaned over to get a better look. The man was clearly a professional acrobat; a man of magnificent physique, with

his huge arms folded across
his massive chest and a smile
breaking from under his heavy
moustache – the self-satisfied
smile of a man who had
achieved much.

'Leonardo, the strongman,
who gave evidence?'

'The same. And this – this is
my husband.'

She then passed us the
second photograph. It was

a dreadful, vicious face that glared back at us. I could imagine that vile mouth foaming in rage, and those small, evil eyes darting pure menace as they looked upon the world. Ruffian, bully, beast – it was all written on that heavy-jowled face.

'Those two pictures will help you, gentlemen, to understand the story. I was a poor circus girl brought up on the sawdust and doing springs through the hoop before I was ten. Once I was grown up I learned that that this man wanted to marry me,' our storyteller gestured to the second picture, 'and out of pity, or weakness, I agreed. From that day I was in hell, and he was the devil who tormented me. There was no one in the show who did not know of his mistreatment. He deserted me for others and whenever I confronted him about it, he would treat

me very cruelly. I often had
to hide bruises. All the other
performers pitied me and
loathed him, but what could
they do? They feared him,
with good reason.

He was terrible at all times and murderous when he was drunk. Again and again he was taken to court for assault and for cruelty to the animals, but he had plenty of money and the fines were nothing to him.'

My heart went out to this lady and I cursed the man who had treated her so savagely. I glanced at Holmes and, although I could only see his profile, saw that he too was moved by her story. His hawklike features had softened and his body slumped a little.

'Many of our best performers left us,' she continued, 'and the show began to go downhill. It was only Leonardo and I who stayed – us and Jimmy Griggs, the clown. Poor devil, he didn't have much to be funny about, but he did what he could to hold things together.

'I was in despair. My life was in the hands of this villain and there was nothing I could do to get myself out of it. Then Leonardo and I grew closer. You see what he was like. I know now the poor spirit that was hidden in that splendid body, but compared to my husband he seemed like an angel. He pitied me and helped me, until at last that kindness turned into love. Deep, deep passionate love.

Such love that I had dreamed
of but never hoped to feel.
My husband suspected it but
I think that he was a coward
as well as a bully, and that
Leonardo was the one man he
was afraid of. He took revenge
in his own way by treating me
worse than ever. One night
my cries of despair brought
Leonardo to the door of our
van. He and I talked about our
desperate situation, and soon
we both understood that my

husband was not fit to live.'

She seemed to sense that she might have shocked us. She paused in her story, looking from one of us to the other. Both Holmes and I were fascinated by this strange tale and nodded for her to continue. Mrs Ronder returned her gaze to the picture of Leonardo and continued. Her voice was little more than a whisper.

'Leonardo had a clever,

scheming brain. It was he who
planned it. I do not say that
to blame him, for I agreed to
go along with his plan. But I
would never have had the wit
to think of it. Leonardo
made a weapon – a club.
To the head he fastened
five long steel nails, the
points outwards, with
the same spread as a
lion's paw. This was
to give my husband
his death blow, and

81

yet to look as though it was the lion that had done the deed.

'It was pitch dark when my husband and I went down, as was our custom, to feed the beast. We carried the raw meat with us in a bucket. Leonardo was waiting at the corner of the big van that we would have to pass to reach the cage. He was too slow. We walked past him before he could strike, but he followed us on tiptoe and I heard the crash as the

blow fell. In that
moment I bitterly
regretted what
I had done, but
I had no choice.
I had to play my
part. Running
forward, I undid
the catch that held
the door of the great lion's
cage so that when we raised the
alarm, people would see the
lion standing over my husband,
assume it had escaped and that

it was responsible. I was glad
that at least I did not have time
to see what Leonardo had done.

'Then the terrible thing
happened. You may have heard
how quick these creatures are
to scent human blood, and how
it excites them. Some strange
instinct told the lion instantly
that a human had been killed.
As I opened the door of the
cage it bounded out and was
on me in an instant. Leonardo
could have saved me. If he had

rushed forward and struck the
animal with his club, he might
have stopped it. But instead the
man lost his nerve. I heard him
shout in terror, and then I saw
him turn and run. At the same
instant, the lion's teeth met my

face. Its hot, filthy breath had
already poisoned me, and I was
hardly conscious of the pain.

'With the palms of my
hands I tried to push the great,
steaming, blood-stained jaws
away from me and I screamed
for help. I was aware that the
camp was filled with shouts,
and then I dimly remember
a group of men – Leonardo,
Griggs and the others –
dragging me from under the
creature's paws. That was

my last memory, Mr Holmes, for many a weary month. When I had recovered enough and saw my face in the mirror, I cursed that lion. Oh, how I cursed him! Not because he had taken away my beauty, but

because he had not taken away
my life. I had just one desire,
Mr Holmes, and I had enough
money to fulfil it. It was that I
should cover myself so that my
poor face should not be seen
by anyone, and that I should
live well away from anyone I
knew. That was all that was left
for me to do – and that is what
I have done. A poor wounded
beast that has crawled into its
hole to die. That is the fate of
Eugenia Ronder.'

All three of us sat in silence for some time after the unhappy woman had told her story. Then Holmes stretched out his long arm and took her hand with such sympathy as I had rarely seen him show.

'You have certainly suffered. You have my sympathies.

But there are a few parts to your story that I do not yet understand. What of this man, Leonardo?'

Her expression held a wistfulness that made my heart go out to her. 'I never saw him or heard from him again. Perhaps I have been wrong to feel so bitterly against him. I cannot expect him to love a thing that a lion has left. But a woman's love is not so easily brushed aside. He had left me under the beast's

claws, he had deserted me in my
hour of need – and yet I could
not bring myself to allow him
to be executed as a murderer.
For myself, I cared nothing
what became of me. What could
be more dreadful than my
actual life? But I stood between
Leonardo and his fate and I felt
that I must protect him.'

'And he is dead?'

She handed us a newspaper
clipping.

'I see,' said Holmes, handing

CIRCUS STRONGMAN
DROWNS

Leonardo Corelli (35), circus strongman, drowned yesterday whilst swimming near Margate. The details of the tragedy are not known since there were few people on the beach at the time, but there are no suspicious circumstances.

Mr Corelli was witness to the tragedy at Ronder's Wild Animals Show seven years ago, when the owner was savaged to death and his wife severely mutilated by an escaped lion.

★ LADIES & GENTLEMEN ★
PRESENTING THE SENSATIONAL
RONDER
WITH HIS
★ WILD ANIMALS ★

back the piece of
paper. 'But what did
he do with his five-
clawed club, which is
the strangest and most
ingenious part of our
story?'

'I cannot tell. There is a
chalk pit near where we set
up camp, with a deep green
pool at the base of it. Perhaps in
the depths of that pool …'

'I see. Well, well, it is of
little consequence now. The

case is closed.'

'Quite, Mr Holmes. The case is closed.'

As she said this, Holmes and I got up from our chairs. As I gathered up my hat and coat, I found Mrs Ronder's final words echoing in my mind. There was a strange edge to her voice that hinted at something deeper. I glanced at my companion and saw a frown on his features. He turned swiftly back to her. 'Your life is not your own,' he said,

fixing her with a reproachful
look. 'Keep your hands off it.'

'What use am I to anyone?'

'How can you tell? The
example of patient suffering is
in itself the most precious of all
lessons in an impatient world.'

The woman's answer was
a terrible one. She got to her
feet, raised her veil and stepped
forward into the light. 'I
wonder if you would suffer this
patiently,' she said.

It was horrible. No words

can describe the framework of a face when the face itself has gone. Two living and beautiful brown eyes looked sadly out from that grisly ruin and I was struck by the pain and despair they held. I suspect that Holmes felt similarly, but instead of saying anything further, he merely held up his hands in a gesture of pity and protest, and together we left the room.

We made our way back to Baker Street in silence, the memory of that face etched on our minds. Even in my work as an army doctor, I had rarely seen anything so terrible. Was it any wonder she had thought to end her life?

I did not stay long. The poor lady's story continued to play on my mind, and I could not remain in Holmes' brooding presence any longer. My mind

was filled with thoughts of
Mary and I hurried home as
quickly as I could, although
this was one story I could never
share with my wife.

Two days later, when I
called on my friend, he greeted
me with a solemn nod and
pointed to a small blue bottle
on his mantelpiece. I picked
it up to see a red label on it

warning that the contents were
poisonous. A pleasant smell of
almond hit me as I opened it.

'Prussic acid?' I said.

'Exactly. It came by post. This
message came with it.' Holmes
passed me a neatly written
note.

I send you my temptation.
I will follow your advice.

'I think, Watson, we can guess the name of the brave woman who sent it.'

Brave indeed. And I was glad that her confession had given her the strength to carry on living.

***

Prussic acid

A deadly liquid, also called hydrogen cyanide, often used in murders and suicides. Easily identified by a pleasant almond scent. Victims often have a faint blue tint to their skin.

In the 19th century it was used in men's aftershave, and fashionable women bathed their eyes in it to enhance their whiteness and brilliancy.

Sherlock Holmes

World-renowned private detective Sherlock Holmes has solved hundreds of mysteries, and is the author of such fascinating monographs as *Early English Charters* and *The Influence of a Trade Upon the Form of a Hand.* He keeps bees in his free time.

Dr John Watson

Wounded in action at Marwan, Dr John Watson left the army and moved into 221B Baker Street. There he was surprised to learn that his new friend, Sherlock Holmes, faced daily peril solving crimes, and began documenting his investigations. Dr Watson also runs a doctor's practice.

To download Sherlock Holmes activities, please visit www.sweetcherrypublishing.com/resources